Measuring Penny

written and illustrated by
Loreen Leedy

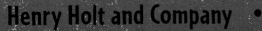

Henry Holt and Company • New York

Henry Holt and Company, LLC, *Publishers since 1866*
115 West 18th Street, New York, New York 10011

Henry Holt is a registered trademark of Henry Holt and Company, LLC

Published in Canada by Fitzhenry & Whiteside Ltd.,195 Allstate Parkway, Markham, Ontario L3R 4T8.

Library of Congress Cataloging-in-Publication Data
Leedy, Loreen.
Measuring Penny / Loreen Leedy.
Summary: Lisa learns about the mathematics of measuring by measuring her dog Penny
with all sorts of units, including pounds, inches, dog biscuits, and cotton swabs.
1. Mensuration—Juvenile literature. [1. Measurement.] I. Title.
QA465.L44 1997 530.8—dc21 97-19108

ISBN 0-8050-5360-3 / First Edition—1997
Typography by Martha Rago
The artist used acrylics on Arches watercolor paper to create the illustrations for this book.
Printed in the United States of America on acid-free paper.∞
10 9 8 7 6 5

For Joyce, who will go the extra mile

Homework:
1) Measure something.
2) Height, width, speed,
   temperature, weight, volume,
3) Record results.

Tanisha

My name is Lisa, and my teacher says our next big homework project is to measure something.

Mr. Jayson says we can measure *anything*—like a sofa,
a television set, or a doll.

Measuring Homework (due next Tuesday!)

1) Choose something to measure.
2) Measure it in as many ways as you can:
   height, width, length, weight, volume,
   temperature, time.
3) Record your results.
4) Include at least one comparison:
   "It is taller than..." or "heavier than..." etc.

Remember, a measurement
always has two parts:
   1) A number
   2) A unit
   "I am 6 feet tall."

Which units can you use?
(Here are some examples.)

Standard Units
inches, feet, yards,
centimeters, meters,
teaspoons, cups, gallons,
pounds, minutes, etc.

Nonstandard Units
paper clips, bricks, frogs,
marbles, pencils, toes, etc.

USE YOUR IMAGINATION!

How tall?
How heavy?
How small?

Measuring helps us to understand
the world.

When I got home today, my dog, Penny, jumped all over me as usual. Wow, I could measure Penny for my homework! She is a Boston terrier, and is bigger than a pug and smaller than a cocker spaniel. She's about the size of a Shetland sheepdog.

(Penny, please stop drooling.)

Shetland Sheepdog

Penny

Pug

Cocker Spaniel

Come on, Penny, I'll get a ruler and we'll run over to the park.

Look at all the dogs out here today . . . hey, get down!

I can't believe how many dogs live around here. Fine, I'll measure some of you, too. We're supposed to use a standard unit, so let me use inches to see how long your noses are . . . stop licking my face!

4 inches
Shetland Sheepdog

1 inch
Penny

1/2 inch
Pug

Lisa

Penny's Measurements

Nose:
  Length = 1 inch
  Unit: inch

Tail:
  Length = 1 dog biscuit
  Unit: dog biscuit

I'll measure your tails with a nonstandard unit—dog biscuits! Will you please hold still? Penny has the shortest tail.

1 dog biscuit
Penny

4 dog biscuits
Fox Terrier

6 dog biscuits
Mixed Breed

10 dog biscuits
Greyhound

I'll measure your ears with another nonstandard unit, cotton swabs. Don't wiggle so much!

Let's see how wide your paw prints are. I'll turn over my ruler and measure with another standard unit, centimeters.

5 centimeters
Mixed Breed

2 ½ centimeters
Dachshund

3 centimeters
Penny

Penny's Paw Print:

Width = 3 centimeters
Unit: centimeter

4 centimeters
Cocker Spaniel

I want to see how tall you all are.
Everybody SIT!

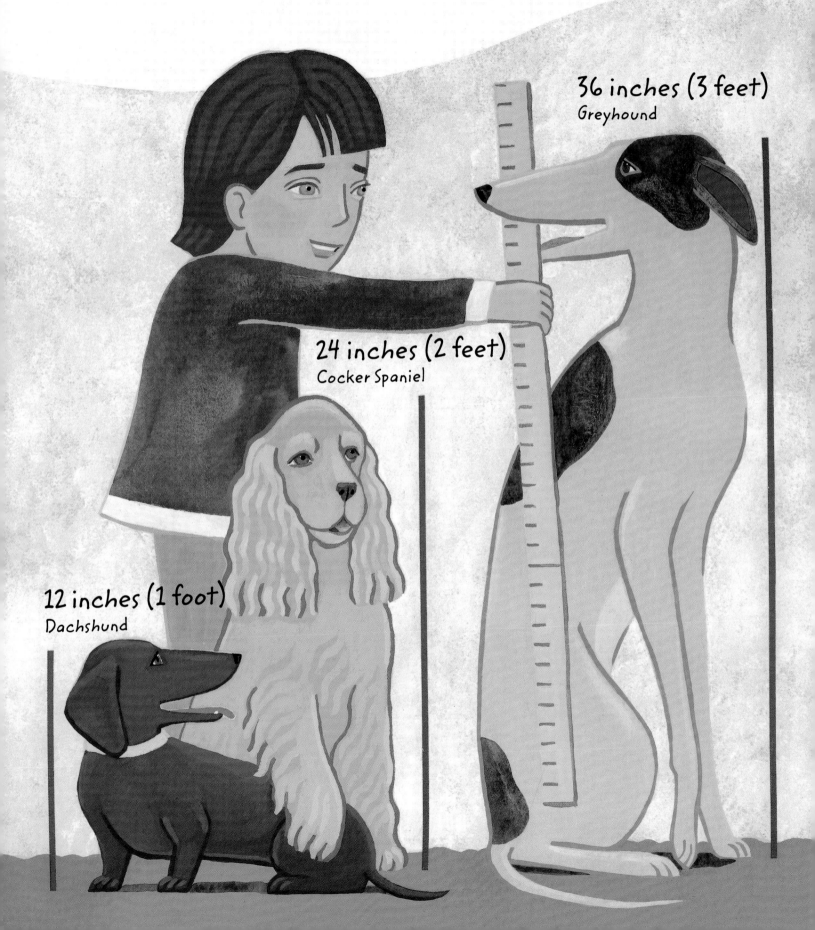

36 inches (3 feet)
Greyhound

24 inches (2 feet)
Cocker Spaniel

12 inches (1 foot)
Dachshund

48 inches (4 feet)
Mixed Breed

Penny's Height:
18 inches
Unit: inch

12 inches = 1 foot
Penny is 1 1/2 feet tall.

3 feet = 1 yard
Penny is 1/2 yard tall.

18 inches (1 1/2 feet)
Penny

Let's see how high you can jump. Penny can jump
up to my waist! I could use *myself* to measure with. . . .

Over My Head

Shoulder-high

Fox Terrier

Waist-high

Knee-high

Basset Hound

There is no scale here in the park, so I can't weigh anything. Wait! I could use the seesaw to see how heavy Penny is compared with the other dogs. The seesaw is down on Penny's end, so she is heavier than the pug.

Weight Comparison

Penny is:

Heavier than the Pug.

Lighter than the Cocker Spaniel.

Same as the Shetland Sheepdog.

Now Penny's end is up because she is lighter than the cocker spaniel.

The seesaw is balanced, so she weighs about the same as the Shetland sheepdog.

You look thirsty, Penny. We'd better go home and get you a drink.
See you later, everybody!

Let's stop in the bathroom so I can weigh you. Get on the scale . . . you're
exactly sixteen pounds. Now let's go to the kitchen for your drink.

Penny's Weight:
16 pounds
Unit: pound

Mr. Jayson says "volume" is the amount of space something fills, like water in a cup. So what *volume* of water do you want? A cup, a pint, a quart, or a gallon? Maybe a tablespoon or teaspoon?

You drank a cup of water already today and I'll give you another cup now. I suppose you're hungry, too.

No, you can't have the whole bag of dog food! I'll give you half a cup.

Sometimes Dad and I make homemade dog biscuits. We measure the ingredients so they taste good (at least to you-know-who).

Doggie Delights
2 cups flour
1/4 cup cornmeal
2 tablespoons melted butter
1 teaspoon bonemeal

I'm going to follow Penny around all day Saturday to measure how much time I spend taking care of her.

Penny's Time Schedule

6:00 a.m.	Wake up.
6–7:00	Patrol house.
7:00	Bark to wake up everybody.
7:05	Take quick walk.
7:10	Eat breakfast.
7:20	Beg for scraps.
8:00	Howl when Mom goes out.
8:10	Take nap.
8:45	Nibble dog biscuits.
12 noon	Eat lunch.
12:15	Take nap.
1:00	Gnaw bone.
1:15	Investigate weird noise in basement.
2:00	Snooze for a while.
2:30	Bark, run in circles.
2:35	Go for a long walk.
3:45	Carry newspaper in.
4:00	Watch cartoons.

I'll make a poster for this part...

Taking Care of Penny
How Much Time Does It Take?

Every day

Feeding her	10 minutes
Brushing her	15 seconds (she has short hair)
Walking her	5 minutes in the morning
	30 minutes in the afternoon
	10 minutes at night
Playing with her	1/2 hour to 1 hour

Weekly

Giving her a bath	15 minutes to 1 hour
Clipping her toenails	5 minutes

Units: hours, minutes, seconds

I'll measure how quickly Penny can run to different places.
She can get from her bed to the kitchen in six seconds!

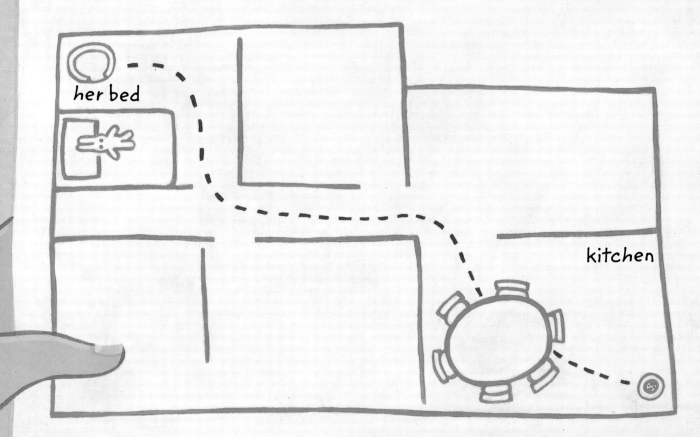

Penny's Breakfast Dash

Penny's Times

Her bed to her dish	6 seconds
Across the backyard	4 seconds
Around the block	5 minutes
To the park	7 minutes
To my bus stop	15 seconds

Units: minutes, seconds

Temperature is important to Penny. She doesn't like things that are too hot . . . or too cold.

Penny likes to go on longer walks when the weather is nice.

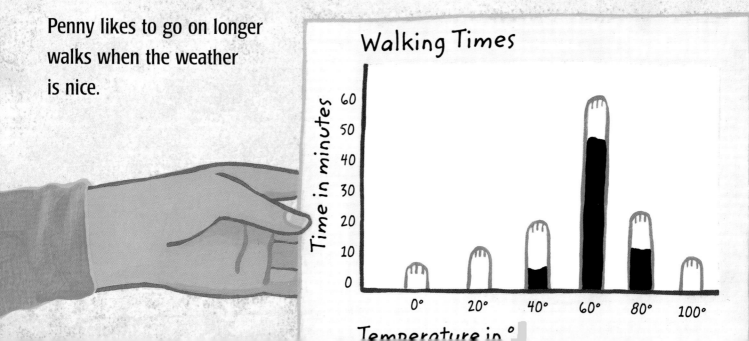

Walking Times

Time in minutes

60
50
40
30
20
10
0

0°   20°   40°   60°   80°   100°

Temperature in °

In fact, you can almost tell the temperature outside just by looking at her.

Penny the Thermometer

80°

60°

40°

20°

0°

Unit: degrees Fahrenheit

The last thing I'm going to measure Penny with is money. Mom looked through her checkbook to help me figure this out. We decided Penny is kind of expensive . . .

Cost of Having Penny

To buy puppy	$275.00
Food (one year)	$400.00
Vet (one year)	$120.00
Toys, collar, etc.	$75.00

Units: dollars, cents

Value of Having Penny

As burglar alarm	$1,000.00
As exercise machine	$500.00
As entertainment	$20.00/day
For LOVE	A million dollars!

Units: dollars, cents

I'm sure Mr. Jayson will give me a good grade on this measuring project. Penny, maybe we should change your name to Million!

ILLAHEE ELEMENTARY